BLAST OFF GRATITUDE!
AN ASTRONAUT'S JOURNAL

with Nova 'Starburst' and friends

BY DANIELLE A. BUTLER
'Captain Cosmic Danielle'

ISBN: 978-1-0670029-2-3

LiftBound books may be purchased for educational, business, or sales promotional use.
For more information, please email Special Markets at hello@LiftBound.net.

For permission requests, write to the publisher at: LiftBound Publishers, hello@LiftBound.net
ISBN: 978-1-0670029-2-3   First Printing: February 2024

Blast Off Gratitude! An Astronaut's Journal, by Danielle A. Butler.
Cover Design and Interior Design: by Danielle A. Butler.
GRATITUDE EXPLORES COLLECTION VOL.2

Disclaimer: The activities, prompts, and suggestions provided in this journal are for personal growth and self-care purposes.
The authors and publisher are not liable for any consequences resulting from the use
or application of the information contained herein.

AI Image Disclaimer: To comply with copyright law, it should be noted that certain images in this
publication have been generated by artificial intelligence and subsequently edited.
These images are subject to the same restrictions outlined above.

Please note that the space images in this journal may not be entirely accurate as our understanding of our universe is
constantly evolving. While we aim to provide accurate representations with a touch of the illustrator's imagination,
they are based on current knowledge and may not reflect the latest scientific discoveries.

This Journal Belong To:

THE BOLDEST ASTRONAUT OF THE COSMIC EXPANSE

Take heed, any interstellar traveler caught exploring it
without authorization shall be jettisoned
into the boundless cosmos of gratitude!

EMBARK ON A COSMIC QUEST!
START EXPLORING AND CHART YOUR COURSE

Greetings, intrepid space explorer! Welcome to your cosmic journal, where our journey to uncover the mysteries of gratitude among the stars begins! Gratitude is like a beacon of light in the endless cosmic sea, guiding us to newfound wonders.

Gratitude goes far beyond a simple "thank you". It's like embarking on a thrilling quest across the universe of your heart each day. It's about discovering the most awe-inspiring moments in your life, from cherished friendships to breathtaking cosmic phenomena, and feeling the boundless joy they bring.

Now, picture this: gratitude is akin to a grand cosmic adventure, where you're not in search of earthly riches but rather moments that make your heart race. And guess what? This journal is your trusty starship on this incredible expedition!

Each day, you'll stumble upon cosmic clues and record them here. Then, at the end of the week, you'll possess a star-chart brimming with celestial smiles!

So, are you prepared to embark on this daring journey across the cosmos? Let's launch our starship and explore the universe together in pursuit of gratitude's mysteries!

P.S. For additional guidance on navigating this Cosmic Quest, explore the rear section of the journal!

Nova 'Starburst' and friends

COSMIC EXPLORATION

Unearth the meteorites of gratitude along your path.

DAY 1: _____ DATE: _____

TODAY, I SOARED THROUGH THE STARS AND FOUND GRATITUDE IN...

1. _____

2. _____

3. _____

PPK

NASA

4. TODAY WAS GREAT BECAUSE
Draw or write something

FACT: All astronauts bring their own PPK when they go into space. PPK stands for Personal Preference Kit. They are personal items which can include things like photos, momentos, flags and patches.

I SHARED SOMETHING I APPRECIATE WITH SOMEONE TODAY BY...

_____

_____

_____

_____

DAY 2: _____ DATE: _____

WHAT I TREASURED MOST TODAY IN THE COSMOS WAS...

1. _____

2. _____

3. _____

4. TODAY WAS GREAT BECAUSE
Draw or write something

Cassette Tape

FACT: The Apollo 9 Astronauts (USA, 1969) could bring one cassette tape each to listen to music. They had to use special cassette players that were modified to prevent the tapes from coming undone in zero gravity.

TODAY I FELT PROUD WHEN I DISCOVERED...

_____

_____

_____

_____

DAY 3: _____ DATE: _____

IN THIS VAST GALAXY I DISCOVERED GRATITUDE FOR...

1. _____

2. _____

3. _____

TENNESSEE
University Pennant

4. TODAY WAS GREAT BECAUSE
Draw or write something

FACT: Astronaut Rhea Seddon, who went on three Space Shuttle trips (USA 1985, 1991, 1993), brought a pennant from her university, a pin from her sorority, a baseball cap from a sports team, and a roll of calculator tape with signatures from students in her hometown.

TOMORROW I'M EXCITED TO EXPLORE MORE ABOUT...

_____

_____

_____

_____

FACTS: Did you know?...
The term 'astronaut' derives from
the Greek words meaning 'star sailor'.

In April 1961, Yuri Gagarin
from the Soviet Union (now Russia)
became the first human
in space aboard Vostok 1.

Cosmonaut Aleksey Leonov, also from the Soviet Union,
was the first person to walk in space.
On 18 March, 1965, he exited his craft
and floated for 10 minutes!

DAY 4: _____ DATE: _____

I SET MY SIGHTS ON TODAY'S GRATITUDE WHICH WAS...

1. _____

2. _____

3. _____

Harmonica

4. TODAY WAS GREAT BECAUSE
Draw or write something

FACT: In December 1965, astronauts Walter 'Wally' Schirra and Tom Stafford brought a harmonica and bell on Gemini 6 (USA), marking the first musical instruments in space. They played Jingle Bells during their mission.

A HEARTWARMING ACT OF COSMIC KINDNESS I EXPERIENCED TODAY

WAS... _____

_____

_____

_____

DAY 5: _____   DATE: _____

TODAY, THE COSMIC WAVES OF GRATITUDE BROUGHT ME...

1. _____

2. _____

3. _____

35mm Camera

4. TODAY WAS GREAT BECAUSE
Draw or write something

FACT: John Glenn's 1962 Mercury Mission (USA) stands out as one of the most iconic. On board, he had a Minolta Ansco Autoset 35mm camera bought from a drug store. It was quickly modified to allow him to use it while wearing his spacesuit.

TODAY, I PUT IN MY BEST LUNAR-TASTIC EFFORT BY LEARNING

ABOUT... _____

_____

_____

DAY 6: _____ DATE: _____

TODAY'S HIDDEN GEM OF GRATITUDE IN SPACE AND BEYOND WAS...

1. _____

2. _____

3. _____

4. TODAY WAS GREAT BECAUSE
Draw or write something

Gorilla Suit

FACT: A retired NASA astronaut, Mark Kelly, sent his twin brother Scott, who was on the International Space Station (ISS) for nearly a year (2015-16), a surprise. He secretly smuggled a gorilla suit aboard the station. One day, Scott put it on and scared British astronaut Tim Peake.

MY JOURNEY INTO KINDNESS CONTINUED TODAY AS I...

_____

_____

_____

_____

DAY 7: _____ DATE: _____

YOUR SPACE ODYSSEY NAME

Hey there, space explorer! It's time to create your very own cosmic name, one that shines as bright as the stars and embodies the spirit of gratitude. Grab your trusty pen and let's embark on this cosmic journey.

1. Start by choosing a quality about yourself that makes you proud. It could be 'Curious', 'Brave', or 'Kindhearted'.

_____

2. Next, think of a space-related object, activity or hobby that brings you joy – it could be 'Galaxy', 'Star', or 'Stargazing'.

_____

3. Finally, add an honorary title, such as 'Commander', 'Captain', or 'Navigator'.

_____

Once you've blended these cosmic ingredients, you'll have your very own space explorer name.
Record it on your Star Map, for this name will guide you on your incredible gratitude journey across the cosmos!

Nova 'Stardust'

NOVA'S GALAXY WORD SEARCH

Are you set for a word search quest to uncover all the celestial wonders you've gathered on your cosmic journey so far? When you spot a word, circle it just like a space explorer charting a new galaxy.

T	X	A	O	E	Y	E	E	N	T	R	A	E	E
H	E	T	A	U	E	S	R	E	V	I	N	U	R
S	N	A	G	G	T	D	E	V	S	B	E	T	O
R	G	S	R	A	I	I	S	T	M	T	E	H	L
T	I	T	A	D	C	L	A	E	R	S	E	A	P
R	M	R	T	I	L	E	O	T	F	K	K	N	X
L	U	O	I	S	S	V	G	E	U	S	R	K	E
N	H	N	T	C	R	N	T	M	E	Y	T	F	O
O	S	A	U	O	A	E	Y	O	B	X	O	U	N
T	M	U	D	V	T	B	H	C	N	A	M	L	O
B	S	T	E	E	S	U	T	A	N	L	T	T	R
E	G	T	A	R	S	L	E	T	A	A	T	S	E
R	K	S	I	Y	R	A	R	B	A	G	L	A	A
C	U	U	H	E	N	E	N	X	E	T	Y	N	N

ASTRONAUT
UNIVERSE
EXPLORE
GRATITUDE
STARS
THANKFUL
NEBULA
GALAXY
COMET
DISCOVERY

Stuck? Clues are at the back

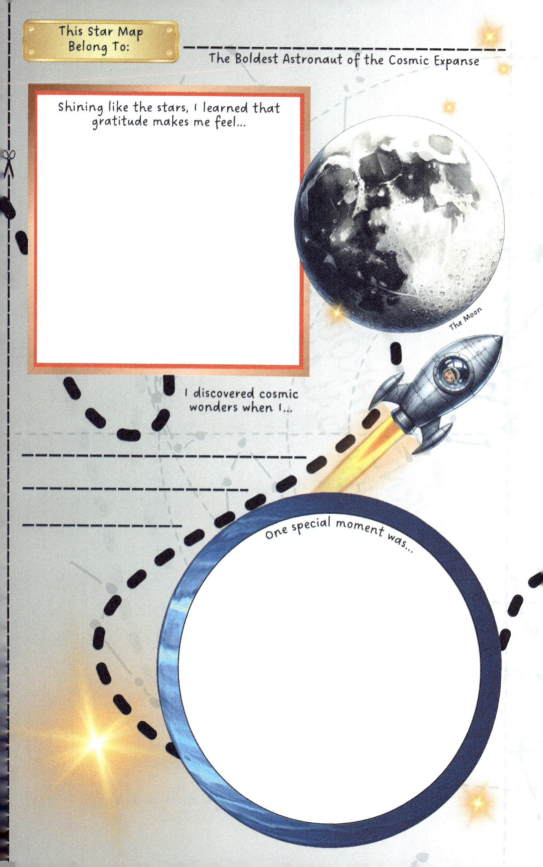

This Star Map Belong To:

The Boldest Astronaut of the Cosmic Expanse

Shining like the stars, I learned that gratitude makes me feel...

The Moon

I discovered cosmic wonders when I...

One special moment was...

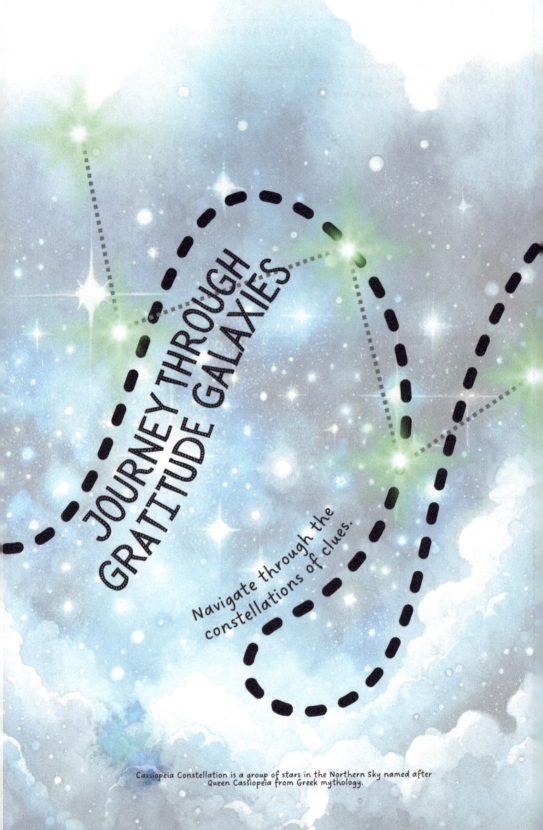

JOURNEY THROUGH GRATITUDE GALAXIES

Navigate through the constellations of clues.

Cassiopeia Constellation is a group of stars in the Northern Sky named after Queen Cassiopeia from Greek mythology.

DAY 8: _____ DATE: _____

TODAY, MY HEART IS AS BIG AS A PLANET WITH GRATITUDE FOR...

1. _____

2. _____

3.

4. TODAY WAS GREAT BECAUSE
Draw or write something

IMAX Camera

FACT: An IMAX camera flew on 12 Space Shuttle missions in the 1980s and 1990s. Astronauts were trained to use it and act as cinematographers to capture footage for IMAX feature films.

I EXPLORED NEW GRATITUDE GALAXIES TODAY BY...

_____

_____

_____

_____

DAY 9: _____ DATE: _____

IN TODAY'S SHINING STARS OF MEMORIES, I'M THANKFUL FOR...

1. _____

2. _____

3. _____

4. TODAY WAS GREAT BECAUSE
Duct Tape   Draw or write something

I HAD A BLAST TODAY WHEN I...

_____

_____

_____

_____

DAY 10: _____ DATE: _____

THE COSMIC TREASURE I FOUND TODAY WAS...

1. _____

2. _____

3. _____

ORBIT OPS CHECKLIST

Checklists

4. TODAY WAS GREAT BECAUSE
Draw or write something

FACT: Astronauts undergo extensive training in classrooms and simulators to prepare for various scenarios, with lots of checklists ensuring successful missions.

TODAY, I FELT A BIT NERVOUS WHEN...

_____

_____

_____

_____

Various things have been left
behind on the moon like...

The Apollo landers had
to launch off the moon and
to accommodate the weight of the
Moon rocks brought back by
astronauts, they left behind
unnecessary items.

Apollo 16 astronaut Charles Duke
left a framed family photo,
and hit and left
two golf balls.

The Moon Museum was left during the
Apollo 12 mission in 1969. It is a small ceramic
wafer containing artworks by six prominent artists
from the late 1960s. It was created by Forrest Myers.

GROSS OR INTERESTING?
There are 96 bags of
human poop on the moon
left behind by the six
Apollo missions (1961-1972).

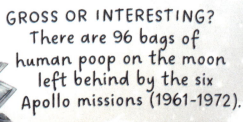

Scientists want to study
the poop, to understand
how lunar conditions
have affected it.

The United States of America has given the Apollo
landing site and the artifacts left there
'Heritage' status (and that includes the poop).

DAY 11: _____ DATE: _____

I MADE EXTRA AWESOME DISCOVERIES TODAY, WHICH WERE..

1. _____

2. _____

3. _____

Fisher.Space Pen

4. TODAY WAS GREAT BECAUSE
Draw or write something

FACT: The Fisher Space Pen is a durable ballpoint pen designed to work in various conditions, including zero gravity, vacuum, and extreme temperatures. It's been used by NASA and Soviet/Russian astronauts on missions such as Apollo, Shuttle, Mir, and ISS.

I EXPRESSED MY INTERGALACTIC CREATIVITY TODAY BY...

_____

_____

_____

_____

DAY 12: _____   DATE: _____

MY SPIRITS WERE LIFTED TODAY BY THE GALACTIC DISCOVERY IN...

1. _____

2. _____

3. _____

Book **4. TODAY WAS GREAT BECAUSE**
Draw or write something

FACT: Books taken to space include "The Hitchhiker's Guide to the Galaxy" by Douglas Adams (1997), "The War of the Worlds" by H.G. Wells (1969), "2001: A Space Odyssey" by Arthur C. Clarke (1968), and "Dune" by Frank Herbert (1994).

SOMETHING THAT BROUGHT LAUGHTER AT WARP-SPEED TODAY WAS...

_____

_____

_____

_____

DAY 13: _____ DATE: _____

TODAY'S LUNAR-TASTIC GEM OF GRATITUDE WAS...

1. _____

2. _____

3. _____

Guitar

4. TODAY WAS GREAT BECAUSE
Draw or write something

FACT: During his 2013 mission to the International Space Station, Canadian astronaut Chris Hadfield played guitar and recorded a viral cover of David Bowie's "Space Oddity".

I'M THANKFUL FOR A SPECIAL COSMIC MOMENT WITH MY FAMILY TODAY...

_____

_____

_____

_____

SPACE SHIP NAME QUEST!

Hello, cosmic explorers! I'm Zara, the Galactic Guardian, and I'm thrilled to have you join our team. Every great space crew needs space ship with a name that sparkles like a distant stars and radiates gratitude from every corner.

YOUR SPACE SHIP IS YOUR HEART ❤️

Imagine the moments when your heart is filled with joy and gratitude. What color does it shine, like the glow of a comet or the brilliance of a distant galaxy? MY COLOR IS _____

YOUR ❤️ IS YOUR NAVIGATOR

Think of a powerful action word that guides your heart as an adventurer. Is it 'quest', 'explorer', or 'adventurer'? Choose a word that captures your spirit as a space explorer. MY ACTION WORD IS _____

Now, blend these two together, and you'll have the start of a perfect name for your cosmic starship! Feel free to share your ship name with your crew. Your starship is your trusty companion on this gratitude-filled cosmic adventure!

Don't forget to write it down on your Star Map!

ZARA'S SECRET CODE

Zara has sent you a secret message. Can you crack the code?

A	B	C	D	E	F	G	H	I	K	L
🚀	★	📝	♡	✔	☀	📎	🎧	☆	⚡	🕐

M	N	O	P	R	S	T	U	V	W	Y
💡	◈	●	📢	➤	⚠	🌐	⚙	👍	🔍	✐

🕐 ● 👍 ✔   💡 🚀 ⚡ ✔ ⚠   ⚙ ⚠   🌐 🎧 🚀 ◈ ⚡ ☀ ⚙ 🕐

☀ ● ➤   🌐 🎧 ✔   ☀ ➤ ☆ ✔ ◈ ♡ ⚠   🔍 🎧 ●

★ ➤ ☆ ◈ 📎   🎧 🚀 📢 ☆ ◈ ✔ ⚠ ⚠   ☆ ◈ 🌐 ●

● ⚙ ➤   🕐 ☆ ⚙ ✔ ⚠   Stuck? Clues are at the back

Write the message here:

MY SPACE SHIP'S
NAME IS

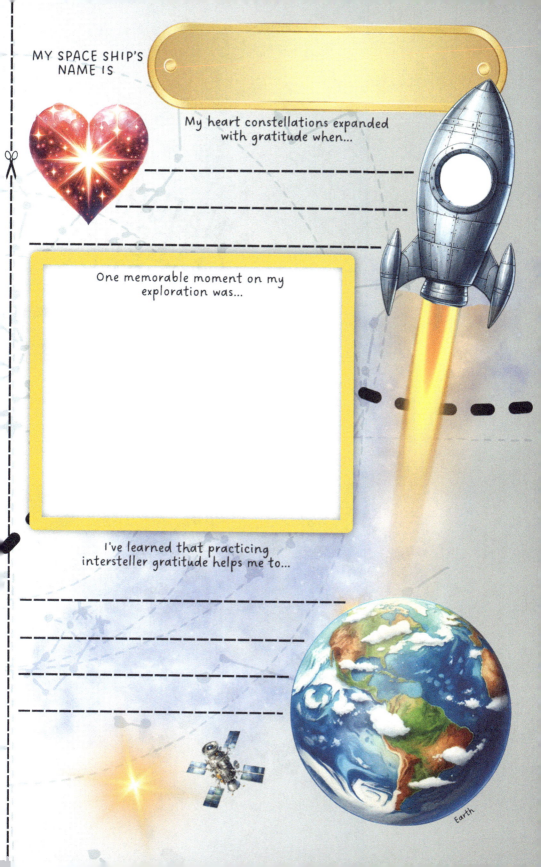

My heart constellations expanded
with gratitude when...

_____

_____

_____

One memorable moment on my
exploration was...

I've learned that practicing
intersteller gratitude helps me to...

_____

_____

_____

_____

Earth

NATURE: CELESTIAL WONDERS

Seek the stardust of appreciation along your voyage.

DAY 15: _____ DATE: _____

TODAY, I HAD AN EXPERIENCE OF GRATITUDE FOR...

1. _____

2. _____

3. _____

4. TODAY WAS GREAT BECAUSE
Draw or write something

Galaxy

FACT: Galaxies vary in shape, including spirals, ellipticals, and irregulars. They typically range in age from 10 to 13.6 billion years old.

I NOTICED SOMETHING BEAUTIFUL IN NATURE TODAY, WHICH WAS...

_____

_____

_____

_____

DAY 16: _____ DATE: _____

THE MOST PRECIOUS COSMIC DISCOVERY I MADE TODAY WAS...

1. _____

2. _____

3. _____

4. TODAY WAS GREAT BECAUSE
Draw or write something

Nebulae

FACT: Nebulae are composed of hydrogen, helium, and dust particles that coalesce due to gravity, increasing in size and gravitational pull over time.

TODAY, I HAD A LOT OF FUN IN NATURE WHEN I...

_____

_____

_____

_____

DAY 17: _____   DATE: _____

TODAY'S VOYAGE IS FULL OF GRATITUDE, ESPECIALLY FOR...

1. _____

2. _____

3. _____

Clusters

4. TODAY WAS GREAT BECAUSE
Draw or write something

FACT: star clusters are collections of hundreds to millions of stars, offering astronomers valuable data on stellar evolution by studying stars' ages and compositions.

I FELT REALLY CALM AND PEACEFUL WHEN I...

_____

_____

_____

_____

FACTS: Did you know?...
The planet Mercury is slightly larger than our Moon.
and it's about 2.6 times smaller than Earth.

Mercury's sun-facing side is scorched by temperatures
430°C, hot enough to melt lead.

Days on Mercury
are very long because
it rotates very slowly.
One day-long spin
lasts for 59 Earth days.

It's the least explored planet.
Only two NASA robotic spacecraft
reached the planet. One in
1974 and the other in 2011.

Earth

Mercury

DAY 18: _____   DATE: _____

IN TODAY'S ADVENTURES, I FOUND GRATITUDE FOR...

1. _____

2. _____

3. _____

4. TODAY WAS GREAT BECAUSE
Draw or write something

Blue stars

FACT: Blue stars appear blue because they emit most of their energy in the bluer parts of the spectrum, which is primarily determined by their high effective temperature.

IN THE HEART OF TODAY'S SPACE ADVENTURE, I'M CHERISHING...

_____

_____

_____

_____

DAY 19: _____   DATE: _____

TODAY I UNCOVERED FOUR COSMIC TREASURES OF GRATITUDE...

1. _____

2. _____

3. _____

Red stars

4. TODAY WAS GREAT BECAUSE
Draw or write something

FACT: Cool stars appear red because most of their energy is emitted in the redder parts of the spectrum, which is primarily determined by their low effective temperature.

I PRACTICED BEING KIND TO NATURE TODAY BY...

_____

_____

_____

_____

DAY 20: _____ DATE: _____

IN THE VAST GALAXY OF TODAY'S MEMORIES I FOUND...

1. _____

2. _____

3. _____

Galaxy   **4. TODAY WAS GREAT BECAUSE**
Draw or write something

I LEARNED SOMETHING NEW ABOUT NATURE TODAY, AND IT WAS...

_____

_____

_____

_____

MY ALIEN'S GRATITUDE PORTRAIT

Riley
Cosmic Crusader

I'm Riley, the Cosmic Crusader, and it's time to grab your pencils. You're going to create a friendly space alien that'll be by your side on this grand odyssey!

Step 1: Close your eyes and imagine how your cosmic companion looks. Is it bursting with colors like a brilliant nebula, or perhaps it shimmers with the silver glow of a far-off star?

Step 2: How does your extraterrestrial friend assist you on your gratitude quest? Does it offer cosmic wisdom when you need guidance? Does it have a playful dance that makes you smile and laugh?

Now, draw a picture of your alien friend. Let your imagination run wild, and don't forget to give them a name that will bring a smile to your face every time you say it!

My Alien Friend's Name is:

_____

I felt amazing when I...

One special moment with nature that made me smile was...

I've learned that being close to nature helps me to...

_____

_____

_____

_____

_____

FACT: 'Green pea' galaxies, discovered in 2009 by the Sloan Digital Sky Survey, are small, round, unresolved dots with a distinct green shade. Rare and compact, they make up only 0.1% of nearby galaxies and have diameters of just 5,000 light-years — 5% of the Milky Way's width.

MISTAKES: INTERSTELLAR LESSONS

Scan the starry expanse for gratitude's cosmic code.

DAY 22: _____   DATE: _____

TODAY'S HIDDEN TREASURE IN MY SPACE ODYSSEY WAS...

1. _____

2. _____

3. _____

Venus

4. TODAY WAS GREAT BECAUSE
Draw or write something

FACT: Decades ago, many scientists mistakenly believed that Venus was mostly covered with water. We now know Venus to be a scorching-hot world with lava flows and potentially active volcanoes.

TODAY, I TRIED MY BEST AT SOMETHING, AND IT WAS...

_____

_____

_____

_____

DAY 23: _____   DATE: _____

EXPLORING THE COSMOS TODAY, I DISCOVERED GRATITUDE IN...

1. _____

2. _____

3. _____

4. TODAY WAS GREAT BECAUSE
Draw or write something

Moon

FACT: Originally, it was believed that the craters on the Moon were formed by volcanic activity. The idea that they could be caused by falling meteorites was not widely accepted. After lots of debates and scientific discovery, it's now understood that while there has been extensive volcanism on the Moon, the craters are not volcanic.

I FELT A LITTLE BIT SCARED TODAY WHEN I...

_____

_____

_____

_____

DAY 24: _____ DATE: _____

BLAST OFF! TODAY I FOUND SOMETHING SPECIAL, WHICH WAS...

1. _____

2. _____

3. _____

Pluto

4. TODAY WAS GREAT BECAUSE
Draw or write something

FACT: Back in 2006, scientists changed the rules for what makes a planet a planet. Poor Pluto got the boot from being a planet to being called a dwarf planet. They decided that to be a planet, something has to do three things: go around the sun, be round like a ball, and not have other things like it nearby. Pluto is missing that last part, so it's now called a dwarf planet. But some people still think Pluto should be a planet, so there's still a big argument about it.

I MADE AN INTERSTELLAR MISTAKE TODAY BUT I LEARNED...

_____

_____

_____

_____

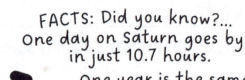

FACTS: Did you know?...
One day on Saturn goes by
in just 10.7 hours.

One year is the same
as 29 Earth years.

Four robotic spacecraft
have visited Saturn, including
Pioneer 11, Cassini, and Voyager 1 and 2.

Voyager 1 showed us Saturn
had over 100 rings!

Saturn doesn't have a true surface.
The planet is mostly swirling
gases and liquids deeper down.

It is made mostly of
hydrogen and helium.

Saturn's magnetic field is
578 times more powerful
than Earth.

DAY 25: _____ DATE: _____

IN MY COSMIC JOURNEY, I STUMBLED UPON GRATITUDE FOR...

1. _____

2. _____

3. _____

4. TODAY WAS GREAT BECAUSE
Draw or write something

Bernard's Star

FACT: In the early 1960s, an astronomer claimed to have found a planet around Barnard's Star. The discovery was accepted without question and even appeared in textbooks until it was disproved in 1973. It turned out that what they thought was a planet was just a mistake caused by a problem with their telescope's lens.

I TURNED A NOT-SO-GREAT FEELING INTO A HAPPY ONE WHEN I...

_____

_____

_____

_____

DAY 26: _____ DATE: _____

STARSHIP SUCCESS! MY HEART IS FILLED WITH GRATITUDE FOR...

1. _____

2. _____

3. _____

4. TODAY WAS GREAT BECAUSE
Draw or write something

Mars

FACT: The Mars Climate Orbiter, launched in 1998, was intended to explore Mars from orbit and relay communications for other missions. It failed due to a navigation error because measurements were not properly converted from English units to metric units. Last contact with the spacecraft was on September 23, 1999, and an investigation found that the spacecraft burned up in Mars' atmosphere.

I PRACTICED BEING KIND TO MYSELF TODAY BY...

_____

_____

_____

_____

DAY 27: _____ DATE: _____

IN TODAY'S COSMIC LOG, I'M THANKFUL FOR...

1. _____

2. _____

3. _____

New glasses
for Hubble?

4. TODAY WAS GREAT BECAUSE
Draw or write something

FACT: The initial images sent by the Hubble Space Telescope were blurry due to an error in the primary mirror. To fix this issue, NASA and ESA constructed additional corrective mirrors, which were installed by astronauts during a special mission. These 'spectacles' successfully corrected Hubble's vision, enabling it to capture clear views of the universe.

SOMETHING I'M GRATEFUL FOR ABOUT MY MISTAKES TODAY IS...

_____

_____

_____

_____

DAY 28: _____   DATE: _____

Riley
Cosmic Crusader

Life is like a cosmic journey, filled with lots of twists and turns. Occasionally, we may stray off course, but that doesn't mean the voyage is over. In truth, sometimes the most cosmic treasures we find are one step further, or hidden at the end of a challenging path.

Like the vast universe, where stars guide us, you need to trust your heart (your starship) to help you navigate the maze of life.

WRITE ABOUT A JAM

Share a cosmic tale from this week when you embarked on an unexpected journey or found yourself in a jam. What occurred and how did you navigate through it? Or perhaps, think about what other cosmic routes you might have taken with your newfound wisdom about the maze of life.

_____

_____

_____

_____

_____

_____

RILEY'S MAZE

You'll need your cosmic intellect and your smarts to get through this maze.

And don't forget, even when you take a cosmic detour, there's always a chance to uncover a hidden planet on the way!

start

Stuck? Clues are at the back

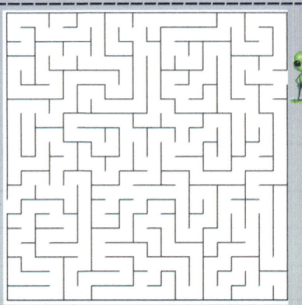

I learned that making a mistake can be an interstellar lesson because...

———————————————————
———————————————————
———————————————————
———————————————————
———————————————————

WASP-104 b

One moment when I made a mistake but discovered gratitude was...

FACT: WASP-104 b is a big gas planet found circling a star like our Sun. It's about 1.3 times the mass of Jupiter and takes only 1.8 days to go around its star. It's pretty close to its star, about 4 million kilometers away, and it was found in 2014. Scientists think it might look purple, but they're not sure yet.

I've learned that mistakes are a secret discovery to become better at...

———————————————————
———————————————————
———————————————————

GALACTIC FEELINGS

Decrypt the interstellar messages of thankfulness.

DAY 29: _____ DATE: _____

TODAY I GOT A COSMIC HIGH-FIVE WHEN I...

1. _____

2. _____

3. _____

Space Dust

4. TODAY WAS GREAT BECAUSE
Draw or write something

FACT: Every day, lots of stuff falls to Earth from space. About 14 tonnes of space dust land on our planet each day. When you're outside, some of this dust might land in your hair. You've probably already caught some, even if you didn't notice!

I FELT REALLY LOVED TODAY WHEN...

_____

_____

_____

_____

DAY 30: _____ DATE: _____

SPACE-TASTIC! TODAY I FOUND GRATITUDE IN...

1. _____

2. _____

3. _____

4. TODAY WAS GREAT BECAUSE
Draw or write something

Earth

FACT: In our galaxy, the Milky Way, there might be around 10 billion planets like Earth. Astronomers used data from space telescopes to find this out. They think about one out of every six stars could have a planet like ours where life could exist.

I NOTICED SOMETHING BEAUTIFUL TODAY THAT MATCHED HOW I FELT, WHICH WAS... _____

_____

_____

_____

DAY 31: _____   DATE: _____

IN THE HEART OF TODAY'S SPACE QUEST, I'M EMBRACING...

1. _____

2. _____

3. _____

4. TODAY WAS GREAT BECAUSE
Draw or write something

saturn

FACT: Saturn has very thin rings made of trillions of ice and rock pieces. They range from tiny dust to big boulders.

TODAY I WAS PROUD OF MYSELF BECAUSE...

_____

_____

_____

_____

FACTS: Did you know?...
There are possibly more trees on Earth
than stars in the Milky Way.

But there are most likely more stars than all
the people ever born on earth.

Just as Earth orbits the sun,
our solar system orbits the
center of the Milky Way.

Lying at the very heart of the Milky Way is a
supermassive black hole called Sagittarius A.

DAY 32: _____   DATE: _____

TODAY'S FLIGHT PATH WAS FILLED WITH GRATITUDE FOR...

1. _____

2. _____

3. _____

Asteroid **4. TODAY WAS GREAT BECAUSE**
Draw or write something

FACT: Asteroids can have moons too! In 1993, NASA's Galileo spacecraft found Dactyl, a small moon orbiting asteroid Ida. This discovery showed that asteroids can have their own moons.

SOMETHING THAT MADE ME LAUGH TODAY WAS...

_____

_____

_____

_____

DAY 33: _____   DATE: _____

TODAY, I UNCOVERED THREE STELLAR TREASURES OF GRATITUDE...

1. _____

2. _____

3. _____

4. TODAY WAS GREAT BECAUSE
Draw or write something

Oumuamua

FACT: In 2017, an unusual object called 'Oumuamua' was spotted by astronomer Robert Weryk in Hawaii. It came from outside our Solar System and was shaped like a cigar. Its visit sparked a big debate about where it came from, and we're still curious about its origins today.

I PRACTICED BEING KIND TO SOMEONE'S FEELINGS TODAY BY...

_____

_____

_____

_____

DAY 34: _____ DATE: _____

TODAY, I UNEARTHED PLANETARY GRATITUDE FOR...

1. _____

2. _____

3. _____

4. TODAY WAS GREAT BECAUSE
Diamonds Draw or write something

FACT: Diamonds, the hardest material on Earth, aren't just found here. They can form in the atmospheres of planets like Uranus and Neptune. Under the right conditions, hydrocarbons in these atmospheres turn into diamonds.

I LEARNED SOMETHING NEW ABOUT MY EMOTIONS, AND IT WAS...

_____

_____

_____

_____

EMOTIONS STAR MAP

Hey crew! Below is a list of different emotions that we all feel at different times. Think about an activity or experience you've had recently and choose the emotion that best describes how you felt during that time.

You might wonder, why do this? Well, understanding our emotions is like exploring the cosmos. It helps us learn more about ourselves and discover which activities bring us joy and which might need some changes. By paying attention to our feelings, we can make better choices on our grand journey through life.

EMOTIONS   ACTIVITY

1. EXCITED   _____

2. HAPPY   _____

3. CURIOUS   _____

4. NERVOUS   _____

5. PROUD   _____

6. FRUSTRATED _____

NOVA STARDUST'S MIGHTY WORD SEARCH

Get ready go on a mighty word search to uncover all the emotions you've discovered so far. Grab a pencil and let the hunt begin!

P	D	O	U	T	R	L	S	S	R	S	A	C	A
E	U	A	A	E	R	U	S	A	S	U	P	C	P
D	N	E	R	V	O	U	S	L	E	R	X	P	Y
P	D	R	L	S	P	R	Y	U	R	P	N	A	R
G	G	Y	L	G	E	E	S	G	Y	R	E	E	G
A	I	P	H	R	E	G	A	D	I	I	P	O	N
A	P	P	D	A	X	G	A	T	G	S	I	A	A
E	E	A	S	T	C	E	E	R	N	E	E	D	U
R	S	H	A	E	I	T	Y	C	A	D	Y	F	Y
R	E	C	U	F	T	E	H	S	D	U	O	R	P
D	D	E	A	U	E	A	C	A	P	C	S	V	M
T	Y	S	F	L	D	X	S	R	S	R	U	U	S
R	S	E	U	E	M	A	M	Y	S	R	R	A	S
D	O	G	P	F	S	C	A	R	E	D	C	D	D

NERVOUS
EXCITED
SAD
SURPRISED
HAPPY
CALM
ANGRY
PROUD
SCARED
GRATEFUL

Nova 'Stardust'

Stuck? Clues are at the back

I was overwhelmed with happiness when...

Draw or write something that makes you happy...

FACT: Uranus is an ice giant in our solar system, along with Neptune. It's mostly made of water, methane, and ammonia, with a small rocky core at the center.

Uranus

I've learned that understanding my feelings brings me closer to...

_____

_____

_____

_____

COSMIC ABILITIES

You are the cosmic key to gratitude's treasures.

DAY 36: _____ DATE: _____

TODAY, I SOARED THROUGH THE STARS AND FOUND GRATITUDE IN...

1. _____

2. _____

3. _____

White Dwarf

4. TODAY WAS GREAT BECAUSE
Draw or write something

FACT: White Dwarfs are stars that are at the end of their life cycle. They happen when stars aren't big enough to become neutron stars or black holes. Most of the stars in our galaxy, the Milky Way, become White Dwarfs when they're old.

I USED MY SPECIAL TALENT TODAY, AND IT WAS...

_____

_____

_____

_____

DAY 37: _____ DATE: _____

TODAY WHAT I TREASURED MOST IN THE COSMOS WAS...

1. _____

2. _____

3. _____

4. TODAY WAS GREAT BECAUSE
Draw or write something

Neutron Star

FACT: Neutron stars are what's left after really big stars die. They're super dense and made mostly of neutrons. When a big star dies, it can become either a neutron star or a black hole.

I NOTICED SOMEONE ELSE'S SUPER STAR TALENT TODAY, WHICH

WAS... _____

_____

_____

DAY 38: _____ DATE: _____

IN THIS VAST GALAXY, I DISCOVERED GRATITUDE FOR...

1. _____

2. _____

3. _____

Red Dwarf

4. TODAY WAS GREAT BECAUSE
Draw or write something

FACT: Red Dwarf stars are the tiniest and most common stars in the universe. In our galaxy, the Milky Way, about three out of every four stars are Red Dwarfs.

I FELT REALLY PROUD OF MYSELF TODAY WHEN...

_____

_____

_____

_____

FACTS: Did you know?...
Mars is the fourth planet from the sun
in our solar system. It's one of the most explored.

It's the only planet where we've sent
rovers to roam the alien landscape.

Mars is about half
the size of Earth.

Mars is home to the largest volcano in the solar system,
called 'Olympus Mons'. It's three times taller
than Earth's Mt. Everest and stands
24 Kilometers (14.9 miles) high.

DAY 39: _____ DATE: _____

I SET MY SIGHTS ON TODAY'S GRATITUDE, WHICH WAS...

1. _____

2. _____

3. _____

4. TODAY WAS GREAT BECAUSE
Draw or write something

Protostar

FACT: A Protostar is like a baby star. It's super young and still growing by collecting stuff from its space cloud. This is just the start of its journey to become a full-fledged star.

SOMETHING THAT MADE ME LAUGH TODAY WAS...

_____

_____

_____

_____

DAY 40: _____ DATE: _____

TODAY, THE COSMIC WAVES OF GRATITUDE BROUGHT ME...

1. _____

2. _____

3. _____

Brown Dwarf

4. TODAY WAS GREAT BECAUSE
Draw or write something

FACT: Brown Dwarfs are like the in-betweeners of space! They're not quite as big as a star, but they're bigger than a planet like Jupiter. If something in space is about 15 times heavier than Jupiter, but not as heavy as a small star, it's called a Brown Dwarf by space experts.

I PRACTICED BEING KIND BY SHARING MY COSMIC ABILITIES TODAY,

AND IT FELT... _____

_____

_____

DAY 41: _____ DATE: _____

TODAY'S HIDDEN GEM OF GRATITUDE IN SPACE AND BEYOND WAS...

1. _____

2. _____

3. _____

4. TODAY WAS GREAT BECAUSE
Draw or write something

Blue Giants

FACT: Blue Giants are stars that shine the brightest in the galaxy because they're super hot and massive! They're called Blue Giants because of their scorching temperatures. But because they burn their fuel so fast, they don't live as long as other stars.

I LEARNED SOMETHING NEW ABOUT MY COMIC TALENTS TODAY, AND IT WAS... _____

_____

_____

YOUR TALENT STAR

Let's talk talents and gratitude. Picture a space ship shooting to the stars, loaded with the talents you already have and those you're dreaming about learning someday.

Think about what you are amazing at right now—art, telling stories, running fast, or making people laugh. Those are your talents, the things that make you one-of-a-kind.

Using your imagination, think of the talents you'd like to learn in future, that might be playing an instrument, climbing a mountain, dancing, singing, or riding a horse.

Luna 'Galactic Guardian'

Now, write below those talents you're dreaming of learning. They are all part of the cargo on your space ship.

_____

_____

_____

_____

_____

_____

GALACTIC WORD SCRAMBLE

Here's another puzzle to help you discover words about the talent stars and skills. Unscramble the letters to find words that showcase your incredible abilities and gifts.

Stuck? Clues are at the back

I A G M A N Z _____.

T C E R A E _____.

T D N E T E A L _____.

S P E A I C L _____.

A E T R G _____.

T A T R S I _____.

I've learned that sharing my talents brings happiness to both me and others by...

_____

_____

_____

_____

FACT: As of March 7th 2024, the satellite tracking website 'Orbiting Now' lists 9,494 active satellites in various Earth orbits.

One amazing moment when I used my special talent was...

I realized how grateful I am for my special talent, which is...

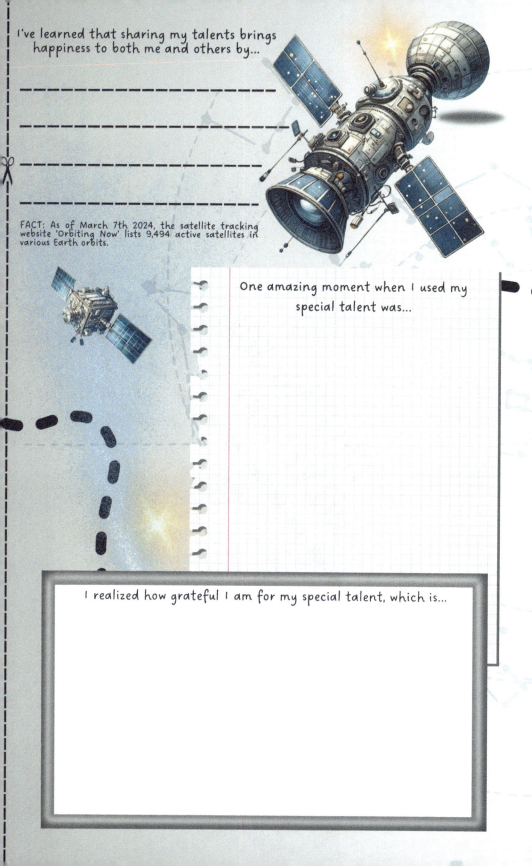

HELPING SOMEONE: UNIVERSAL KINDNESS

The constellations hold clues to cosmic thankfulness.

Aries is one of the constellations of the zodiac. It is located in the Northern celestial hemisphere between Pisces to the west and Taurus to the east. The name Aries is Latin for ram.

DAY 43: _____ DATE: _____

TODAY, MY HEART IS AS BIG AS THE SUN WITH GRATITUDE FOR...

1. _____

2. _____

3. _____

Microscope

4. TODAY WAS GREAT BECAUSE
Draw or write something

FACT: Biology, physiology, fluid physics and combustion, material sciences, fundamental physics and astrobiology are all studied in space

I SPRINKLED STAR DUST AND HELPED SOMEONE TODAY BY...

_____

_____

_____

_____

DAY 44: _____ DATE: _____

IN TODAY'S SHINING STARS OF MEMORIES, I'M THANKFUL FOR...

1. _____

2. _____

3. _____

plants

4. TODAY WAS GREAT BECAUSE
Draw or write something

FACT: Scientists on the International Space Station (ISS) are studying how plants grow in space through an experiment called C4 Space. They're looking at how they capture carbon dioxide. This helps us understand how plants grow in space and could help us create life support systems for future missions.

ASTRO-AWESOME! SOMEONE HELPED ME TODAY AND IT FELT...

_____

_____

_____

_____

DAY 45: _____ DATE: _____

THE BRIGHT COSMIC TREASURE I FOUND TODAY WAS...

1. _____

2. _____

3. _____

Atomic Clock

4. TODAY WAS GREAT BECAUSE
Draw or write something

FACT: The International Space Station (ISS) are doing experiments with Atomic Clock Ensembles in Space (ACES) which helps scientists study gravity and sync clocks worldwide. It uses atomic clocks in space to do cool experiments, like measuring atoms and searching for dark matter. This helps us understand physics better!

I NOTICED A KIND THING SOMEONE DID FOR ME TODAY, WHICH WAS...

_____

_____

_____

_____

FACTS: Did you know?...
One million Earths could
fit inside the Sun and
the Sun is considered
an average-size star.

On Dec. 14, 2021 NASA's
Parker Solar Probe flew through the
Sun's upper atmosphere - the corona.
It's the first time in history
a spacecraft touched the sun!

Our Sun is a 4.5 billion-year-old
Yellow Dwarf star in the
middle of our Solar System.

The temperature of the Sun
is between 5,973°C to 15,000,000°C
That's 10,783°F to 27,000,032°F.

DAY 46: _____ DATE: _____

I MADE EXTRA AWESOME DISCOVERIES TODAY, WHICH WERE..

1. _____

2. _____

3. _____

Petrie Dish

4. TODAY WAS GREAT BECAUSE
Draw or write something

FACT: The International Space Station (ISS) are doing experiments with BioNutrients. It's a project that creates nutrients for astronauts during long space missions from special microbes like yeast to make healthy stuff called carotenoids. They supplement potential vitamin losses from food that is stored for very long periods.

SOMETHING I'M GRATEFUL FOR ABOUT HELPING OTHERS TODAY IS...

_____

_____

_____

_____

DAY 47: _____ DATE: _____

MY SPIRITS WERE LIFTED TODAY BY THE GALACTIC DISCOVERY IN...

1. _____

2. _____

3. _____

skeleton

4. TODAY WAS GREAT BECAUSE
Draw or write something

FACT: Bone loss is a big problem for astronauts in space. The International Space Station (ISS) is doing a study called Bone on ISS to learn more about it. They check bone health before, during, and after spaceflight to see how it changes.

I PRACTICED BEING KIND BY HELPING TODAY, AND IT FELT...

_____

_____

_____

_____

DAY 48: _____   DATE: _____

TODAY'S SUN BEAMS OF GRATITUDE WERE...

1. _____

2. _____

3. _____

4. TODAY WAS GREAT BECAUSE
Draw or write something

Camera

FACT: Astronauts on the International Space Station (ISS) take pictures of Earth using their own cameras. They're 320 kilometers (200 miles) above the ground, so they get a unique view. These pictures help us see how Earth changes over time, like when cities grow or when there are big storms or volcanic eruptions.

TODAY, I LEARNED HOW HELPING SOMEONE CAN MAKE ME FEEL...

_____

_____

_____

_____

COSMIC KINDNESS

Let's have a chat about helping others and why it's so important. You see, lending a hand to someone is mission critical! Every astronaut works within a team and when they help each other during their missions, great discoveries happen!

Now, here's the real mission: helping someone without expecting anything in return. When you lend a hand, or share a piece of your heart, it's like a shining star. The more you give without wanting anything back, the brighter you are.

So, draw a picture of yourself on a mission - where you are helping someone. It could be helping a friend, picking up trash on the beach (or moon), or sharing something special, or helping your teacher. Draw yourself lending a hand and making someone smile.

Nova & Zara

One special moment when I helped someone and felt really good about it was...

Neptune

FACT: Neptune was the first planet located using math. A day on Neptune is 16 hours. One year on Neptune is about 65 Earth years.

I found cosmic joy in helping someone when...

I've learned that helping others is like finding happiness in...

probe the universe of thanks
for hidden trails.

THE SMALL THINGS

DAY 50: _____ DATE: _____

TODAY, I HAD A ZERO-GRAVITY EXPERIENCE OF GRATITUDE FOR...

1. _____

2. _____

3. _____

4. TODAY WAS GREAT BECAUSE
Draw or write something

TODAY, I NOTICED SOMETHING SMALL THAT MADE ME HAPPY, WHICH
WAS... _____

_____

_____

_____

DAY 51: _____ DATE: _____

THE MOST PRECIOUS COSMIC DISCOVERY I MADE TODAY WAS...

1. _____

2. _____

3. _____

4. TODAY WAS GREAT BECAUSE
Draw or write something

Rehydratable Food

FACT: Astronauts eat rehydratable foods that are made by adding water to them. These foods are made by taking out the water using special methods like freeze drying. They can eat things like rice, noodles, powdered drinks, and even shrimp cocktails by adding water to them.

I FELT REALLY CALM AND PEACEFUL TODAY WHEN...

_____

_____

_____

_____

DAY 52: _____ DATE: _____

TODAY'S VOYAGE IS FULL OF GRATITUDE, ESPECIALLY FOR...

1. _____

2. _____

3. _____

4. TODAY WAS GREAT BECAUSE
Draw or write something

Thermostabilized
Food

FACT: Astronauts also eat foods that come in cans. Some of these foods can be eaten right away, while others need to be heated up in a food warmer. They have things like canned curry, fish, grilled chicken skewers, meatloaf, ravioli, and pudding.

I PRACTICED BEING KIND BY APPRECIATING SMALL THINGS TODAY,

AND IT FELT... _____

_____

_____

FACTS: Did you know?...
Atoms are like tiny building blocks that
make up everything around us.

They have a center called a nucleus,
which is surrounded by even
tinier particles called electrons.

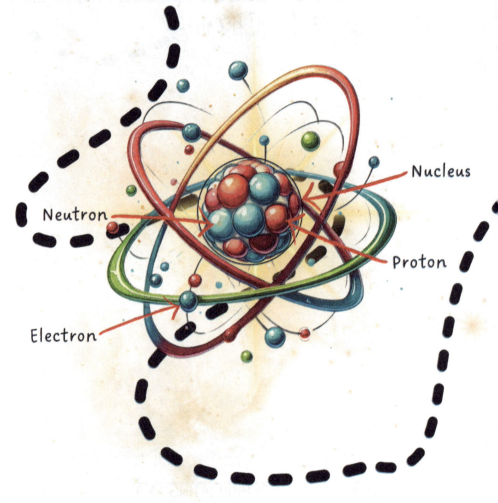

Nucleus

Neutron

Proton

Electron

The nucleus has protons, which are positive,
and neutrons, which are neutral.

Together, they make up all the
stuff we see and touch.

DAY 53: _____ DATE: _____

IN THE HEART OF TODAY'S SPACE ADVENTURE, I'M CHERISHING...

1. _____

2. _____

3. _____

Dried Fruit

4. TODAY WAS GREAT BECAUSE
Draw or write something

FACT: Astronauts also have snacks that are ready to eat, like cookies, candy, and jelly desserts. They can also enjoy dried fruits, tortillas, and beef jerky.

A HAPPY MEMORY I THOUGHT ABOUT TODAY WAS...

_____

_____

_____

_____

DAY 54: _____ DATE: _____

TODAY, I UNCOVERED THREE COSMIC TREASURES OF GRATITUDE...

1. _____

2. _____

3. _____

4. TODAY WAS GREAT BECAUSE
Draw or write something

Liquid Salt

FACT: In space, salt and pepper are turned into liquids to keep them from floating around in the weightless environment.

SOMETHING THAT MADE ME LAUGH TODAY WAS...

_____

_____

_____

_____

DAY 55: _____ DATE: _____

IN THE VAST GALAXY OF TODAY'S MEMORIES, I FOUND...

1. _____

2. _____

3. _____

4. TODAY WAS GREAT BECAUSE
Draw or write something

Mayonnaise

FACT: Yes! Astronauts have mayo in space.

I LEARNED SOMETHING NEW ABOUT FINDING JOY IN SMALL THINGS
TODAY, AND IT WAS...

_____

_____

_____

EXPLORE LITTLE WORLDS

It's time for a little-big adventure in nature to celebrate the small things around us. As explorers, we'll be searching for microcosms.

What's a microcosm? It's a tiny world of something bigger, like a miniature universe. Imagine you are an ant. What would it be like in their world? A small pebble might look like a boulder, a blade of grass a giant tree, and a flower a space ship!

Luna 'Galactic Guardian'

Now, head outside to a park, garden, or your own yard.   Bring paper or your journal and a pencil.

1. **Find it:** Find a miniature world, a microcosm. Look very, very closely.
2. **Observe:** Imagine you were super tiny. What do you see?
3. **Write it Down:** Write about that miniature world. What would it be like to live in that universe? What other creatures are there? What would be fun about it? And what about the dangers? Microcosms are fully of discovery!

_____

_____

_____

_____

_____

_____

THE SPACE SHUTTLE

The Space Shuttle fleet flew 135 missions from 1981 to 2011, and helped contruct the International Space Station (ISS).
How many shuttles do you count?

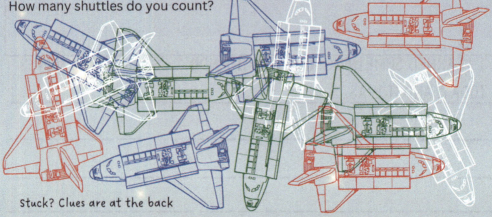

Stuck? Clues are at the back

My Best Find...

I found gratitude in the
small things, like...

I've learned that it's the
little things that make
my universe big because...

_____
_____
_____
_____
_____
_____

FACT: Venus is the second
planet from the Sun and is
Earth's closest neighbor. It's about
the same size as Earth and has a thick
atmosphere that traps heat, making it
the hottest planet in our solar system.

Venus

CELEBRATING ACHIEVEMENTS

Your cosmic compass points to gratitude's wonders.

DAY 57: _____ DATE: _____

TODAY'S HIDDEN TREASURE IN MY SPACE ODYSSEY WAS...

1. _____

2. _____

3. _____

4. TODAY WAS GREAT BECAUSE
Draw or write something

Black Hole

FACT: A black hole is a place in space where gravity is super strong. Nothing, not even light, can escape from it.

TODAY I CELEBRATED A COSMIC ACHIEVEMENT, WHICH WAS...

_____

_____

_____

_____

DAY 58: _____ DATE: _____

EXPLORING THE COSMOS TODAY, I DISCOVERED GRATITUDE IN...

1. _____

2. _____

3. _____

Exoplanet

4. TODAY WAS GREAT BECAUSE
Draw or write something

FACT: Exoplanets are planets that orbit stars outside our solar system. They're tricky to spot because they're overshadowed by the bright light of their stars.

I FELT REALLY PROUD OF MYSELF TODAY WHEN...

_____

_____

_____

_____

DAY 59: _____ DATE: _____

BLAST OFF! WHAT I FOUND SPECIAL TODAY WAS...

1. _____

2. _____

3. _____

4. TODAY WAS GREAT BECAUSE
Draw or write something

Comet

FACT: Comets are remnants from the birth of our solar system around 4.5 billion years ago, made up of sand, ice, and carbon dioxide.

I NOTICED SOMETHING BEAUTIFUL IN MY ACHIEVEMENT TODAY, WHICH WAS...

_____

_____

_____

FACTS: Did you know?...
There is a planet likely
made of diamonds.

40 light-years away from us
is an exoplanet, 55 Cancri e.

Scientists believe at least a third
of the planet's mass (about three
Earth masses) could be diamond.

If true, that's about $26.9 nonillion in diamonds!
$26,900,000,000,000,000,000,000,000,000,000

DAY 60: _____   DATE: _____

IN MY COSMIC JOURNEY, I STUMBLED UPON GRATITUDE FOR...

1. _____

2. _____

3. _____

Space Shuttle

4. TODAY WAS GREAT BECAUSE
Draw or write something

SOMETHING THAT MADE ME LAUGH TODAY WAS...

_____

_____

_____

_____

DAY 61: _____ DATE: _____

STARSHIP SUCCESS! MY HEART FILLED WITH GRATITUDE FOR...

1. _____

2. _____

3. _____

4. TODAY WAS GREAT BECAUSE
Draw or write something

Asteroid

FACT: About once a year, an asteroid the size of a car enters Earth's atmosphere, but thankfully, it burns up before reaching us. Whew!

I PRACTICED BEING KIND TO MYSELF BY CELEBRATING MY
ACHIEVEMENTS TODAY, AND IT FELT...

_____

_____

DAY 62: _____ DATE: _____

IN TODAY'S COSMIC LOG, I'M THANKFUL FOR...

1. _____

2. _____

3. _____

4. TODAY WAS GREAT BECAUSE
Draw or write something

Apollo Foot Print

FACT: Because the moon lacks an atmosphere, there's no wind or water to wash away the marks left by the Apollo astronauts. This means their footprints, rover tracks, spacecraft prints, and other items will remain preserved on the moon for a very long time.

TODAY, I LEARNED HOW IMPORTANT IT IS TO CELEBRATE MY ACHIEVEMENTS BECAUSE...

_____

_____

_____

YOUR ASTRONAUT'S LOCKER OF ACHIEVEMENTS

It's time to celebrate all the fantastic things you've achieved on your gratitude journey, no matter how big or small. Imagine you have a special cosmic locker where you keep all these achievements. We're gonna make one!

1. **Find a Box or Container:** First, find a small box or container for your locker. It can be any size, but make sure it's big enough to hold some discoveries.

2. **Decorate Your Locker:** Get creative! Decorate your locker to make it look like a real astronaut's locker. You can use paints, markers, stickers, or even glue on some pictures.

Riley
'Cosmic Crusader'

3. **Write It Down:** Now, grab some small pieces of paper. On each one, write down one of your achievements. It can be anything you're proud of, like finishing a page in your Astronaut's Journal, helping someone, or something you're proud of.

4. **Fill Your Locker:** Fold up each piece of paper with an achievement written on it and place it inside your locker. As you add more achievements, your locker will fill up with your very own discoveries and treasures!

Celebrate! Whenever you feel like celebrating, or when you need a reminder, open your locker and read about all the amazing things you've accomplished. Remember, every achievement, no matter how small, is worth celebrating!

Draw a picture of your locker:

One memorable moment when I celebrated something important to me was...

_____

_____

_____

_____

Jupiter

I celebrated a cosmic milestone, which was...

FACT: Jupiter is the biggest planet in our solar system. It is more than twice as massive as all the other planets combined.

I've learned that celebrating my achievements helps me to...

_____

_____

_____

_____

Zero-gravity high-five!

THE FINAL VOYAGE

DAY 64: _____ DATE: _____

TODAY I GOT A COSMIC HIGH-FIVE WHEN I...

1. _____

2. _____

3. _____

THROUGHOUT THIS GRATITUDE JOURNEY
I'VE DISCOVERED THAT...

BLAST OFF! I'M AMAZING AT...

_____

_____

_____

_____

DAY 65: _____ DATE: _____

SPACE-TASTIC! I KNOW HOW TO FIND GRATITUDE IN...

1. _____

2. _____

3. _____

A SPECIAL MOMENT DURING
MY GRATITUDE JOURNEY WAS...

THE SILLIEST THING THAT HAPPENED WAS...

_____

_____

_____

DAY 66: _____ DATE: _____

MY FLIGHT PATH OF GRATITUDE LED ME TO...

1. _____

2. _____

3. _____

I'VE LEARNED THAT GRATITUDE
HAS MADE ME FEEL...

MY HAPPIEST ADVENTURE WAS...

_____

_____

_____

_____

FACTS: Did you know?...
Earth, our home, is the third planet from the Sun and the fifth largest. It's the only known place with life.

Earth's atmosphere is made up of 78% nitrogen, 21% oxygen, 1% other.

Earth is unique because a large portion of its surface is covered in liquid water, thanks to temperatures that support its existence for long durations.

You live on an amazing planet!

DAY 67: _____ DATE: _____

I UNEARTHED PLANETARY GRATITUDE FOR...

1. _____

2. _____

3. _____

I'VE LEARNED THAT THIS JOURNEY HAS
HELPED ME BECOME MORE AWARE OF...

THE BEST SURPRISE I'VE HAD LATELY IS...

_____

_____

_____

_____

DAY 68: _____ DATE: _____

I REACHED ZERO-GRAVITY IN GRATITUDE BY...

1. _____

2. _____

3. _____

I PRACTICED KINDNESS AND GRATITUDE BY...

THE FRIENDLIEST THING SOMEONE DID FOR ME DURING MY QUEST
WAS...

_____

_____

_____

DAY 69: _____ DATE: _____

I INCREASED MY NEBULA KNOWLEDGE OF GRATITUDE BY...

1. _____

2. _____

3. _____

MY GRATITUDE JOURNEY HAS TAUGHT ME THAT...

IF I COULD GIVE A HIGH-FIVE TO ANYONE IN THE WORLD,
IT WOULD BE... _____

_____

_____

_____

CELESTIAL ODYSSEY: BEYOND THE STARS

Your whole crew is here to give you the biggest congratulations for completing this journal! You've shown the heart of a true adventurer, discovering the stars, comets, and quasars of gratitude day by day.

Remember, my cosmic explorer, that this journey is unique to you. No matter where the galaxies of life take you, what adventures you encounter, or what extraterrestrial life you meet, you've learned how special you are. Each day is a new chance to see the universe through grateful eyes.

Now, below, you'll find a space to jot down how you feel, or you can get a head start on drawing your beautiful gratitude galaxy on the next page. So go ahead, my fellow star traveler, prepare to make your mark and let your light shine like the brightest star in the cosmos. Your gratitude adventure continues!

In my astronaut's locker I now have...

_____

_____

_____

_____

_____

When I look back on my gratitude journey I realized...

_____

_____

_____

_____

_____

_____

_____

My next cosmic quest is...

_____

_____

_____

_____

STUCK? NEED HELP WITH CLUES?

If you ever get stuck on the puzzles, don't worry. We've got the solutions right here to help you out! Try not to look...

DAY 7: NOVA'S GALAXY WORD SEARCH

DAY 35: NOVA STARDUST'S WORD SEARCH

DAY 14: ZARA'S SECRET CODE

Love makes us thankful for the friends who bring happiness into our lives.

DAY 42: GALACTIC WORD SCRAMBLE

AMAZING
CREATE
TALENTED
SPECIAL
GREAT
ARTIST

DAY 28: RILEY'S MAZE

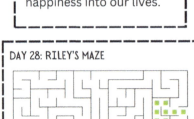

DAY 56: THE SPACE SHUTTLE

12 SPACE SHUTTLES

HOW TO USE THIS JOURNAL: THE PRINCIPALS

*Gratitude is not only the greatest of virtues
but the parent of all others.* - Marcus Tullius Cicero

This guide is for the grown-ups and caregivers who are joining their space explorer on their gratitude journey.

This Gratitude Journal is to help your explorer to embrace genuine moments of gratitude and have some joyful fun along the way! It's all about creating positive impacts in their daily life, and guess what? It's suppose to be an adventure!

Firstly, let's break down 'gratitude'. It's not just about being thankful (like someone opening a door for you). It's a deep, heartfelt appreciation for the good stuff in life. It's about recognizing the goodness, value, and blessings around you, without expecting anything in return.

Now, for this gratitude practice, and for your explorer to have a truly transformative experience, remember these key points:

1. **Be Specific:** Instead of general thanks, be specific about what they appreciate.
2. **Personal Connection:** Focus on what truly matters to them personally.
3. **Understand Why:** Explore why it's meaningful to them. It may seem silly to you, but if it's important to them, don't change it!
4. **It Has a Lasting Feeling:** Gratitude isn't fleeting. It sticks around, making them feel good inside.

This journal offers a structured way to weave gratitude into their routine. It's to be used when their day is mostly over, or done. Then each week's theme builds on the next. The aim is to broaden your explorers personal growth journey. *And yes, you can cut out the last page of the week, tape them together and create a Star Map!*

There are ten weeks, or themes, and seventy days. They cover the following themes: Discovery, Exploring Gratitude, Nature, Mistakes, Emotions, Talents, Helping Someone, The Small Things, Celebrating Achievements, and the last theme is on how the gratitude journey is a life long practice.

But here's the golden rule: No forcing! Let your space explorer set their own pace. The journal is meant to be enjoyable, not a homework assignment or chore. Although it would be great to complete a page daily, please go at the pace of your explorer. They may need more time to think, process and absorb their gratitude journey.

As you dive into this adventure of self-reflection, intention, and personal growth, you'll discover the beauty of their imagination. So grab your space suit, and catch a rocket into this cosmos of gratitude, and let the adventure begin!

'Captain Cosmic Danielle'

GRATITUDE EXPLORERS COLLECTION

Ready to embark on another thrilling journey of gratitude and self-discovery? Dive into another adventure with our Gratitude Explorers Collection and uncover new treasures of happiness and positivity!

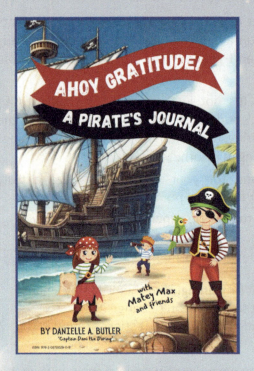

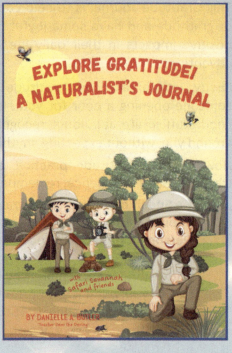

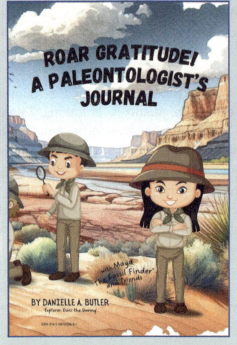

Stay tuned for more themes packed with more fun!

Discover us on Amazon or at your favorite local bookstore!

🌐 LiftBound.net

✉ hello@liftbound.net

📷 @LiftBoundForGood

f LiftBound

Bye!

If you enjoyed this journal, please share it with others and consider
leaving a review on Amazon and share on Social to
help more kids discover the magic of gratitude!

🌐 LiftBound.net   ✉ hello@liftbound.net   (f) LiftBound   © @LiftBoundForGood

ISBN: 978-1-0670029-2-3